IF

YOU'RE

A

MONSTER

AND

YOU

KNOW

IT

Sing along with this book!

To download your free copy of the song
"If You're a Monster and You Know It,"
performed by Adrian Emberley, please go to
www.scholastic.com/ifyoureamonsterandyouknowit.

All rights reserved. Published by Orchard
Books, an imprint of Scholastic Inc.,
Publishers since 1920. Orchard Books
and design are registered trademarks
of Watts Publishing Group, Ltd., used under license.
SCHOLASTIC and associated logos are trademarks
and/or registered trademarks of Scholastic Inc.

Library of Congress Cataloging-in-Publication Data is available.
ISBN 978-0-545-21829-0
10 9 8 7 6 5 4   11 12 13 14
Printed in Singapore   46
Reinforced Binding for Library Use

First edition, September 2010
The artwork was created using Freehand.
The display text was set in Decaying Kuntry.
The text was set in Iron Latch.
Book design by Rebecca Emberley

by Rebecca Emberley & Ed Emberley

IF YOU'RE A MONSTER AND YOU KNOW IT

ORCHARD BOOKS
An Imprint of Scholastic Inc.

If you're a monster and you know it, snort and growl
If you're a monster and you know it, snort and growl
If you're a monster and you know it,
and you really want to show it,
if you're a monster and you know it – snort and growl

SNORT

If you're a monster and you know it, smack your claws
If you're a monster and you know it, smack your claws
If you're a monster and you know it,
and you really want to show it,
if you're a monster and you know it – smack your claws

If you're a monster and you know it, stomp your paws
If you're a monster and you know it, stomp your paws
If you're a monster and you know it,
and you really want to show it,
if you're a monster and you know it – stomp your paws

STOMP

STOMP

STOMP

If you're a monster and you know it, twitch your tail
If you're a monster and you know it, twitch your tail
If you're a monster and you know it,
and you really want to show it,
if you're a monster and you know it – twitch your tail

If you're a monster and you know it, wiggle your warts
If you're a monster and you know it, wiggle your warts
If you're a monster and you know it,
and you really want to show it,
if you're a monster and you know it – wiggle your warts

WIGGLE

If you're a monster and you know it, give a ROAR!
If you're a monster and you know it, give a ROAR!
If you're a monster and you know it,
and you really want to show it,
if you're a monster and you know it – give a ROAR!

ROAR
ROAR
ROAR

If you're a monster and you know it, do it all!

SNORT GROWL

SMACK SMACK

STOMP STOMP

TWITCH TWITCH

WIGGLE WIGGLE

ROAR
ROAR ROAR

If you're a monster and you know it, do it all!

SNORT SMACK STOMP TWITCH WIGGLE ROAR
GROWL SMACK STOMP TWITCH WIGGLE ROAR ROAR

If you're a monster and you know it,
and you really want to show it,

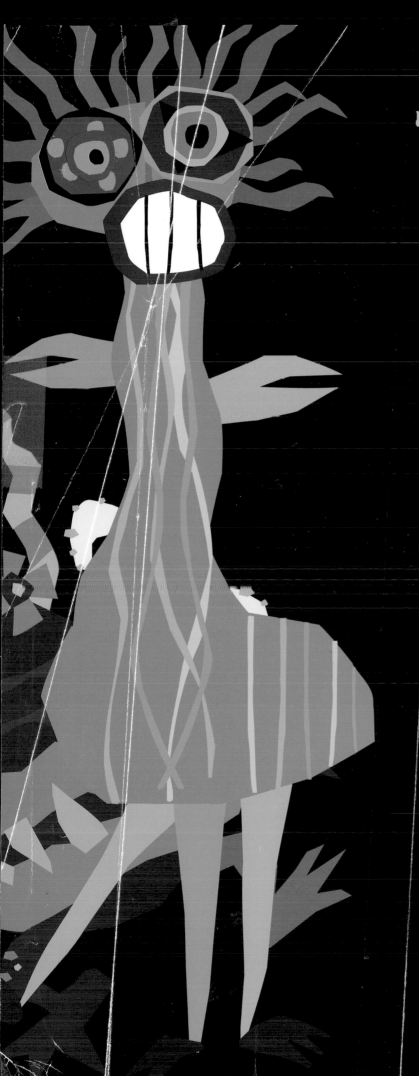

If you're a monster and
you know it – do it all!

SNORT
GROWL

SMACK
SMACK
STOMP
STOMP
TWITCH
TWITCH
WIGGLE
WIGGLE

ROAR
ROAR

If you're a monster and you know it — do it all!

SNORT   SMACK   STOMP   TWITCH   WIGGLE   ROAR
GROWL   SMACK   STOMP   TWITCH   WIGGLE   ROAR

Now, do it again....

DATE			